# CONTENTS

Material based on content originally written by Derek Ritchie
Wizards vs Aliens - created by Russell T Davies and Phil Ford

WIZARDS VS. ALIENS word and device marks are trade marks
of the British Broadcasting Corporation and are used under licence.

WIZARDS VS. ALIENS © BBC 2013

The "BBC" word mark and logo are trade marks of the British Broadcasting
Corporation and are used under licence.  BBC Logo © BBC 1996.
Licensed by FremantleMedia Limited.

Published 2013. Century Books Ltd.
Unit 1, Upside Station Building Solsbro Road,
Torquay, Devon, UK, TQ26FD

info@centurybooks.co.uk

"IT'S WIZARDS VS ALIENS AND I'M READY FOR THEM."

# TOM CLARKE

**Name:** Tom Clarke

**Age:** 16

**Eyes:** Brown

**Hair:** Brown

**Species:** Human wizardkind

**From:** Earth

**Often found:** On the football pitch

**Favourite Spell:** 'Maah-gann dah' (football redirection)

**Likes:** Football, seafood pizza with extra jalapenos and anchovies

**Dislikes:** Homework, Magic-eating aliens

**Additional Info:** Before the Nekross arrived, Tom loved using Magic to make life easier – from ensuring he scored the winning goal to completing his homework in a flash. Wizards are only able to use 3 spells per day and with the threat from the Nekross, he's going to need every one of those spells just to survive.

"THESE ARE ALIENS TOM, THAT'S NOT HOCUS POCUS, IT'S SCIENCE."

# BENNY SHERWOOD

**Name:** Benny Sherwood

**Age:** 16

**Eyes:** Brown

**Hair:** Brown

**Species:** Human

**From:** Earth

**Often found:** The school science lab or the 'Shed of Dread' in his parents' garden

**Favourite Spell:** Benny prefers science to save the day, not Magic

**Likes:** Science experiments – especially explosive ones!

**Dislikes:** Playing sports, Magic-eating aliens

**Additional Info:** School science geek Benny didn't have an easy relationship with Tom until the two were paired up on a history field trip to an ancient stone circle. Their discovery of an enchanted ring set in motion a chain of events which would change their lives and bond Benny and Tom forever.

"CHAMBER OF CROWE, OPEN TO ME, REVEAL YOURSELF ON THE KNOCK OF THREE."

# URSULA

**Name:** Ursula (7th daughter of the 7th daughter of the Magical Line of Crowe)

**Age:** A lady never tells!

**Eyes:** Blue

**Hair:** Grey

**Species:** Human wizardkind

**From:** Earth

**Often found:** In the Chamber of Mysteries (accessed by Magic through the Clarke's downstairs loo.)

**Favourite Spell:** 'Sprash-afalla-waan dah!' (Spring Cleaning)

**Likes:** Tangleweed Tea, brewing Magical potions

**Dislikes:** Technology, particularly mobile phones

**And another thing:** Not the most skillful of spell-casters, Ursula sometimes creates all kinds of chaos with her spells. It's a good job she has Randal Moon at her side, constantly imparting his Magical wisdom.

"YOU KNOW THE RULE - NO SPELLS OUTSIDE HOME!"

# MICHAEL CLARKE

| | |
|---|---|
| Name: | Michael Clarke |
| Age: | 42 |
| Eyes: | Brown |
| Hair: | Black and grey |
| Species: | Human |
| From: | Earth |
| Often found: | At the veterinary practice where he works |
| Favourite Spell: | None. He prefers to do things the Unenchanted way |
| Likes: | Chinese food, animals |
| Dislikes: | The use of Magic to cheat or shirk daily responsibility |

Additional Info: Since the death of his wife, Helen, Michael has been raising son Tom, with mother in law Ursula's help. Uncomfortable around Magic, he does his best to keep Tom's feet on the ground, but will nevertheless do everything he can to help his son in the battle against the Nekross.

"I'LL BE A HOBGOBLIN. HOB! HOB! HOB!"

# RANDAL MOON

**Name:** Randal Moon

**Age:** 500 years and a little bit more!

**Eyes:** Brown

**Hair:** None!

**Species:** Hobgoblin

**From:** Earth

**Often found:** In the Chamber of Mysteries – he is bound to it by Magic

**Favourite Spell:** 'Raa-shey dah!' (Shrouding spell)

**Likes:** The mistress Crowe, answering Magical questions

**Dislikes:** Tecknockery, Unworld ones from the evil Sky-Boat

**And another thing:** Randal Moon is the Guardian of the Chamber and has dwelled there for over 500 years. Ursula is his best friend and Mistress and he helped teach her the ways of Magic when she was a little girl. He now does the same for young Master Tom.

# FRIENDS

Although the burden of his responsibility to wizardkind and to Earth, weighs heavily on Tom's shoulders, he luckily has a large circle of friends on hand to offer help and support. Some are aware of his true 'Magical' nature and of the Nekross threat, whilst others remain blissfully unaware, but all touch Tom's life. Here's a guide to who's who...

## JACKSON HAWKE

| | |
|---|---|
| **AGE:** | 17 |
| **EYES:** | Blue |
| **HAIR:** | Brown |
| **SPECIES:** | Human wizardkind |
| **FROM:** | Earth |
| **OFTEN FOUND:** | Playing computer games |
| **FAVOURITE SPELL:** | Grim Magic Banishment Charm |
| **LIKES:** | Using Grim Magic, Meat Feast pizza |
| **DISLIKES:** | Authority figures, stuffy old wizards |

**ADDITIONAL INFO:** Jackson Hawke is a cool, confident and powerful teenage wizard. He has harnessed the dangerous powers of Grim Magic to free himself from the confines of life with his parents. Having Magically banished them he now does exactly what he wants. Jackson enthralls Tom, but the pair soon discover that Grim Magic comes at a price.

## HELEN CLARKE

| | |
|---|---|
| **AGE:** | 35 |
| **EYES:** | Blue |
| **HAIR:** | Brown |
| **SPECIES:** | Human wizardkind |
| **FROM:** | Earth |
| **OFTEN FOUND:** | 'Beyond the veil', but her 'pale shadow' may return to warn her family of danger |
| **FAVOURITE SPELL:** | 'Mah-shaan-zah-dah!' (Destroys Nekross technology) |
| **LIKES:** | Saving her family and the world! |
| **DISLIKES:** | Magic-eating aliens, missing Tom growing-up |

**ADDITIONAL INFO:** Helen was a brave wizard. She died on Halloween night 2006, protecting her son Tom from a Nekross Probe which collected her DNA. This led to the Nekross' attempt to clone a never-ending supply of wizards for Magic extraction.

# "TOM SEEMS SUCH A NICE BOY, AND HE'S BENNY'S FRIEND...AT LAST!"

## RICHARD AND TRICIA SHERWOOD

| | |
|---|---|
| **AGE:** | Very middle-aged! |
| **EYES:** | Brown |
| **HAIR:** | Black |
| **SPECIES:** | Human |
| **FROM:** | Earth |
| **OFTEN FOUND:** | Relaxing in their comfortable home |
| **LIKES:** | Having family quiz nights, speaking French, playing classical music |
| **DISLIKES:** | Popular culture, TV of any sort, processed food |

**ADDITIONAL INFO:** Richard and Tricia Sherwood are the archetypal middle-class pushy parents, desperate for their son Benny to succeed academically. Richard is a mathematical and software genius and owns a technology company, which allows him and his family to live very comfortably. They are big on organic food and ecology and have a sustainable multi-fuel boiler in the basement – which is almost responsible for the destruction of Tom and Benny, when the Grazlax turns up.

## QUINN CHRISTOPHER

| | |
|---|---|
| **AGE:** | 16 |
| **EYES:** | Brown |
| **HAIR:** | Blond |
| **SPECIES:** | Human |
| **FROM:** | Earth |
| **OFTEN FOUND:** | Kicking a football around the playground or park |
| **LIKES:** | Football |
| **DISLIKES:** | School and nerds who like school |

**ADDITIONAL INFO:** Football mad Quinn has been pals with Tom for years, their friendship forged on the football pitch and cemented by Tom's 'Magical' talent for scoring. With Tom no longer wasting spells on

## KATIE LORD

| | |
|---|---|
| **AGE:** | 16 |
| **EYES:** | Brown |
| **HAIR:** | Brown |
| **SPECIES:** | Human |
| **FROM:** | Earth |
| **OFTEN FOUND:** | On her bike – delivering leaflets for her Dad's shop |
| **LIKES:** | Tom Clarke, bowling |
| **DISLIKES:** | Football |

**ADDITIONAL INFO:** Katie goes to King's Park School with Tom and Benny. She'd love to go out with Tom and the feeling is mutual. Pretty, funny and confident, she even manages to get him on a date to the cinema; only to be stood up when he sees someone he thinks

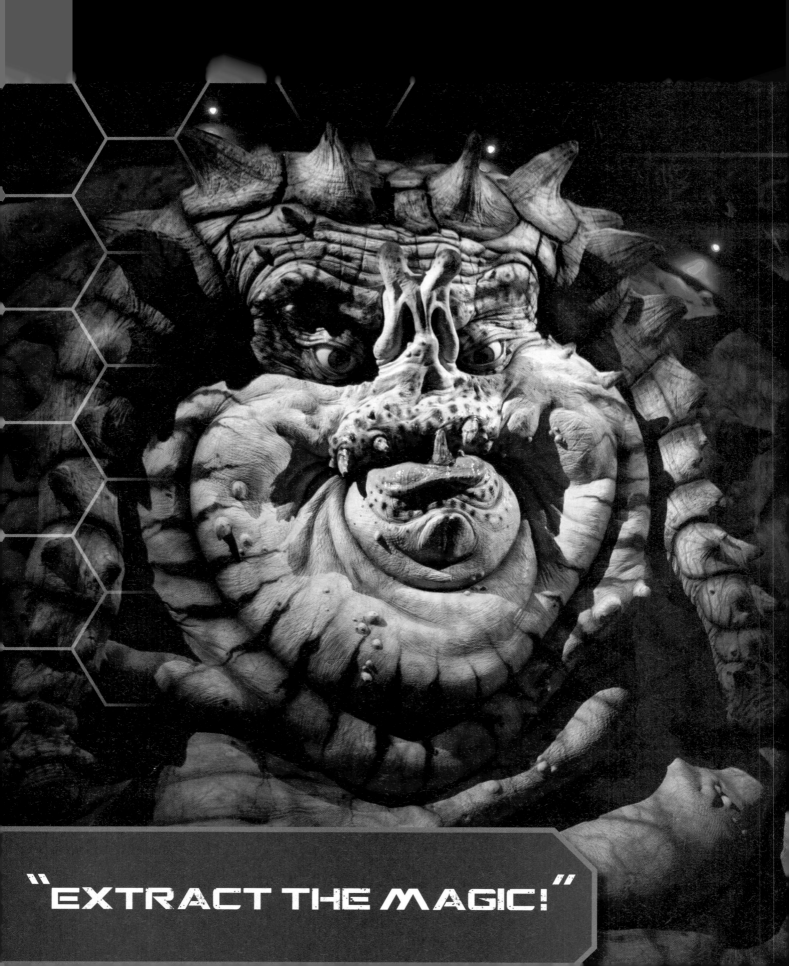

"EXTRACT THE MAGIC!"

# THE NEKROSS KING

**NAME:** The Nekross King

**AGE:** Unknown

**APPEARANCE:** Corpulent and generally repulsive

**SPECIES:** Nekross

**FROM:** The planet Nekron in the Korbol galaxy

**OFTEN FOUND:** In his recess on the Flight Deck of the starship Zarantulus

**LIKES:** Feasting on Magical energy, keeping his royal warts moist

**DISLIKES:** Failure, hunger

**ADDITIONAL INFO:** The Nekross value nothing more than the sweet taste of freshly extracted Magical energy. The King has consumed so much of it that his body has swollen to gargantuan proportions. Now completely immobile, the Magic must be piped directly into his recess so that he can feast. The King is so greedy that he becomes enraged if he is not fed and his offspring Varg and Lexi know that they must provide food – or perish!

"EVERY STAR, WHERE THERE WAS ONCE MAGIC, NOW BURNS DIMMER."

# VARG

| | |
|---|---|
| **NAME:** | Varg. Prince of Nekron |
| **AGE:** | Unknown |
| **APPEARANCE:** | Tall, scaly and intimidating |
| **SPECIES:** | Nekross |
| **FROM:** | The planet Nekron in the Korbol galaxy |
| **OFTEN FOUND:** | On the Flight Deck of the starship Zarantulus or hunting wizards on Earth |
| **LIKES:** | Capturing wizards, being heir to the throne, using disintegrating blasters on his foe |
| **DISLIKES:** | Disgusting humans, Lexi's superior intelligence |

**ADDITIONAL INFO:** As first-born son of the Nekross King Varg is next in line to the Nekron throne, a position in which he revels. Varg is a fearsome warrior, in possession of terrifying advanced technology, who has fought his way through the universe in the quest for Magic. He has captured many wizards and extracted their Magic to feed his family.

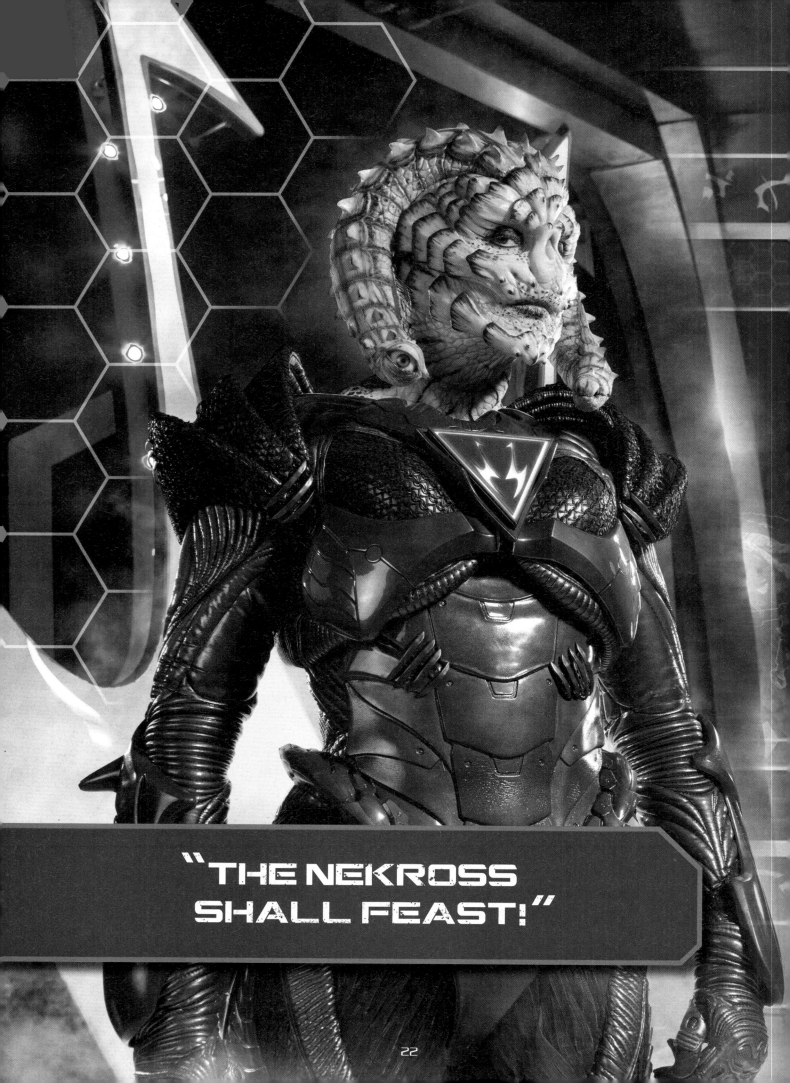

"THE NEKROSS
SHALL FEAST!"

# LEXI

**NAME:** Lexi. Princess of Nekron

**AGE:** Unknown

**APPEARANCE:** No less scaly or intimidating than her brother

**SPECIES:** Nekross

**FROM:** The planet Nekron in the Korbol galaxy

**OFTEN FOUND:** On the Flight Deck of the starship Zarantulus or hunting wizards on Earth

**LIKES:** Extracting Magic, hatching cunning plans, finding out about other planets

**DISLIKES:** Disgusting humans, Varg showing her up

**ADDITIONAL INFO:** Lexi is the proudly loyal daughter of the Nekross King and is a very clever adversary. While she lacks the brawn and military prowess of her brother, she more than makes up for this with brainpower, using strategy and cunning to hunt out wizards. She knows that understanding your enemy and their weaknesses can lead to a swifter victory and has spent time on Earth disguised as a human called 'Lucy'.

# FOES

The Nekross Royal Family is not the only threat to Tom and his friends – and the Earth in general. From megalomaniac businesswomen bent on world domination to terrifying, fanged fur-balls which will destroy anything in their path, many creatures are also vying to cause chaos and catastrophe.

## THE GRAZLAX

| | |
|---|---|
| **AGE:** | Unknown |
| **APPEARANCE:** | Blue fur-ball, with enormous, sharp fangs, a horn and red eyes |
| **SPECIES:** | Grazlaa |
| **FROM:** | Grazlaxicon III, in the Korbol galaxy |
| **OFTEN FOUND:** | Anywhere they are sent by the Nekross |
| **LIKES:** | Hunting down victims using scent and then destroying them |
| **DISLIKES:** | High-pitched noise, getting too hot |

**ADDITIONAL INFO:** The Grazlaa are feared throughout the universe as they can munch, smash and tear their way through anything. Having captured one, the Nekross are only able to contain it using a special box made from a dense alloy found in dying stars. The only thing which may keep it at bay is a high-pitched noise. While heat may initially seem to repel a Grazlax, it will in fact only result in an explosion of orange goo and the triple multiplication of the creature. Yikes!

## JATHRO

| | |
|---|---|
| **AGE:** | Unknown |
| **APPEARANCE:** | Red, black and scaly |
| **SPECIES:** | Nekross |
| **FROM:** | The planet Nekron in the Korbol galaxy |
| **OFTEN FOUND:** | On the starship Zarantulus |
| **LIKES:** | Pleasing the Royal family, ingenious technology |
| **DISLIKES:** | Being starved of Magic, being unfit for duty |

**ADDITIONAL INFO:** Technician Jathro Fifteen of sub-section Alpha Grex Nine is a lowly technician-class Nekross on the Zarantulus. Like all Nekross, he craves Magic to eat, but being of a lower class, never gets to enjoy it himself. Instead this sly fawning alien, steadfastly loyal to his King and Royal Highnesses Varg and Lexi, relishes preparing wizards for the Extractor and pulling the lever to extract their Magic.

# STEPHANIE GAUNT

**AGE:** How dare you be so impertinent!

**APPEARANCE:** Expensively groomed and power-dressed

**SPECIES:** Human

**FROM:** Earth

**OFTEN FOUND:** In her office at Gaunt Technologies

**LIKES:** Being in control, being anonymous, getting what she wants

**DISLIKES:** Liars, incompetent staff

**ADDITIONAL INFO:** Ruthless and successful, Stephanie Gaunt's greed knows no bounds. Her vast fortune means she has everything that money can buy and now wants everything money can't buy. She thinks Magic can make this happen and is determined to get it, even if that means kidnap. However she gets more than she bargains for when she unwittingly captures a wizard... and an alien!

# "LET'S START WITH THE WORLD AND THEN, WHY NOT - THE WHOLE UNIVERSE!"

# THREE SPELLS

Human wizards can cast only three spells between sunrise and sunset and with the Nekross threat to Earth, Tom must work with the limitations and use his spells wisely. Pick from the wizarding words below to create your own Magical incantations. Remember a spell will always end with the word 'Dah!' Very powerful spells will end 'Zah-Dah!' Use the opposite page to write out your spells in English and in Stonescript and then explain what they allow you to achieve. Pick one word from each column.

| | |
|---|---|
| AVA | AFALLA |
| AYRA | BELLAK |
| BRAAK | DACH |
| DEESCH | DIGGER |
| DREE | FAA |
| DYSHAA | FALOW |
| EIN | FAN |
| FAYE | FARDACH |
| KADRA | FASHA |
| KALIZ | GANN |
| MAAH | GRAAK |
| MASS | KRAAK |
| MAIFASH | KYFAA |
| MAHDAH | PRACH |
| MEESCH | SEH |
| MYFAA | SHAAN |
| MYSTAH | SHAH |
| RAA | SHATH |
| SHIN | SHEY |
| SPRASH | SHO |
| SPREE | SHOSH |
| TORASCH | TRATH |

Spells end with
## DAH!

Powerful Spells end with
## ZAH-DAH!

## 1

**English** _____

_____

**Stonescript** _____

_____

**Meaning** _____

_____

## 2

**English** _____

_____

**Stonescript** _____

_____

**Meaning** _____

_____

## 3

**English** _____

_____

**Stonescript** _____

_____

**Meaning** _____

_____

# KEY

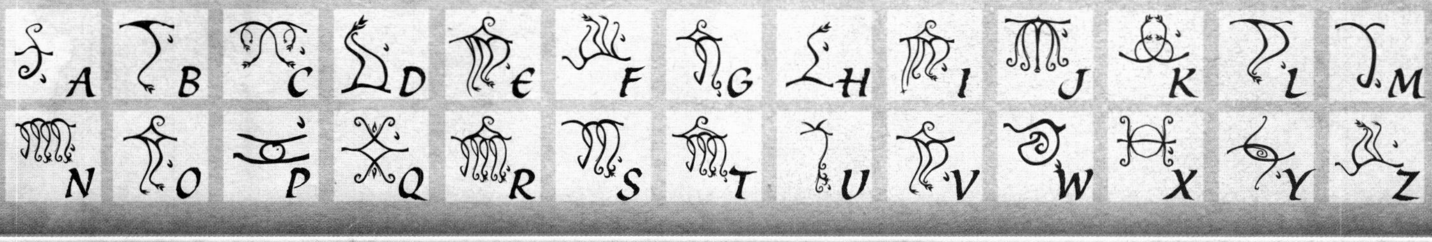

A  B  C  D  E  F  G  H  I  J  K  L  M

N  O  P  Q  R  S  T  U  V  W  X  Y  Z

# NEKROSS YOUR TEACHER!

The Nekross are very fond of possessing human bodies – they temporarily took over teacher Miss Webster using the Voolox! They can also disguise themselves as humans using their Form Filters. Lexi appeared as the human 'Lucy', to try and trick Tom! How would your favourite or worst teachers look as aliens? Give them a Nekross-over!

# BENNY'S BIG QUIZ

Unsuspecting schoolboy geek Benny Sherwood has been somewhat thrown in the deep-end, since he and Tom were paired up on a field trip to a Magical stone circle. Now he finds himself immersed in a world he never knew existed, filled with wizards and malevolent extra-terrestrials, so it's a case of learn fast – or be disintegrated! Test your geek knowledge with the first part of his quiz on the wizarding world.

(1) Wizards have an unlimited number of spells they can cast each day. — True/False

(2) Tom comes from the Magical Line of Rook. — True/False

(3) His grandmother Ursula is the seventh daughter of the seventh daughter of this Magical Line. — True/False

(4) Tom's father has no Magic and is called an 'Unenchanted' by wizards. — True/False

(5) There is a Magical Chamber in Tom's house accessible through the garage. — True/False

(6) The Magical Chamber can be reached by knocking three times and saying a Magical incantation. — True/False

(7) A goblin dwells in the
    Chamber of Mysteries.                    True/False

(8) Randal Moon calls
    Ursula 'the Lady Crowe'.                 True/False

(9) The Wizards can see
    what's happening in the
    wider world through the                  True/False
    pages of a spell book?

(10) The written language of
     Wizards is called Wandscript.           True/False

(11) Wizards who die are said to
     pass 'beyond the veil', where           True/False
     they sleep.

(12) They can return to the world as
     ghosts, when they want to warn          True/False
     someone about something.

(13) The use of Grim Magic is
     dangerous because it is so
     powerful it can eat away at and         True/False
     destroy the Wizard who uses it.

(14) Earth is at risk from the Nekross,
     because they want to settle on
     the planet and see the Wizards          True/False
     as a threat.

Answers on page 92-93

# WIZARD'S WORD SEARCH

Can you locate the wizarding words and phrases listed below in the wordsearch opposite? Make sure you use your powers of observation to search in every direction!

AMBER

CANE

CHAMBER OF MYSTERIES

CHARM

CLOAK

CURSE

ENCHANTMENT

GRIM MAGIC

HOBGOBLIN

LINE OF CROWE

POTIONS

SCRYING MIRROR

SPELL BOOK

STONESCRIPT

TANGLEWEED TEA

THE SOURCE

THE STONES

THREE

UNENCHANTED

VIAL

| N | I | L | B | O | G | B | O | H | P | N | O | T | I | T | D | A | C |
|---|---|---|---|---|---|---|---|---|---|---|---|---|---|---|---|---|---|
| B | U | T | H | R | E | E | G | R | O | I | P | O | T | N | R | H | A |
| S | O | T | H | E | S | E | N | O | T | S | E | H | T | E | A | L | M |
| T | H | O | G | L | S | P | L | L | I | M | R | G | R | M | S | S | R |
| O | N | I | L | S | I | K | E | D | O | N | R | O | B | T | P | T | A |
| N | S | H | R | G | A | N | S | R | N | A | R | E | O | N | L | N | H |
| E | P | R | K | O | R | D | E | E | S | R | R | L | L | A | L | E | C |
| S | E | C | L | O | O | S | R | O | I | O | J | H | B | H | G | L | D |
| C | L | C | O | G | R | E | N | M | F | H | O | B | G | C | A | N | E |
| R | L | I | L | U | A | M | G | M | E | C | H | O | B | N | N | O | T |
| I | B | T | C | R | R | N | Y | N | A | T | R | I | V | E | D | U | N |
| P | O | R | E | E | I | S | H | T | H | E | S | O | U | R | C | E | A |
| T | O | E | G | Y | T | A | H | O | V | I | A | L | W | C | R | P | H |
| S | K | E | R | E | H | B | O | H | T | A | N | G | L | E | E | T | C |
| T | O | C | R | I | E | E | X | T | R | A | C | T | I | O | N | I | N |
| N | S | I | B | R | E | B | M | A | E | O | F | C | R | W | E | N | E |
| E | E | P | O | T | G | R | I | M | M | A | G | I | C | O | U | S | N |
| S | O | T | A | N | G | L | E | W | E | E | D | T | E | A | R | T | U |

"You found all the words? Well done you wonderful child! But there is one challenge left – another word, not listed. This word strikes fear in the hearts of all Wizards. It describes what will happen to us if the Nekross capture us. It's how they steal our Magic."

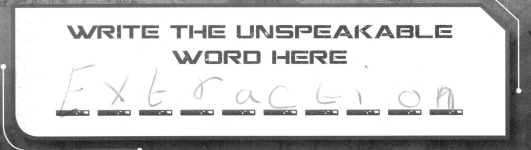

**WRITE THE UNSPEAKABLE WORD HERE**

Extraction

# WHO SAID IT?

Are you wise about Wizards and all clued up about Aliens? Take part in the Quotes Quiz to see how closely you've been watching the action! Simply match the quotes to a character from the show but beware, there may be more than one quote per character!

(1) "Tom Clarke is no friend of mine – I'll cut him down like any other wizard, you will see."

(2) "You have Magic. You have alien science. You're going to tell me how to commit the perfect crime."

(3) "You defy me, wizard? I who have bestrode the stars?"

(4) "It's wizards versus aliens. And I'm ready for them."

(5) "Cat's claws and monkey's paws."

(6) "As you can see, I'm well past my sell-by date!"

(7) "Avengers assemble!"

(8) "At least the hag Crowe has the stomach for war."

(9) "What we've got is so fantastic, because what we've got is power!"

(10) "What? Aliens? What sort of goblin garbage is this? There are no such things as aliens!"

# DAWN OF THE NEKROSS

Tom Clarke stepped off the school bus and blinked in the sunlight. His teacher, Miss Webster was already in full flow.

"Remember, Burnt Hill Stone Circle is a heritage monument... it is neither a climbing frame, nor a Neolithic chalkboard!"

Tom didn't mind being on a history field trip – it was better than being stuck in class – but he'd far rather have been on the football pitch, using one of his three daily spells to score goals. No one but Tom's father and his grandmother, Ursula, knew Tom's secret: he was a wizard.

Walking into the stone circle Tom stopped in his tracks, images flashed through his mind like some terrifying sci-fi movie; two figures – a man and a boy – amid the stones, caught in the teleport beam of an alien spaceship.

"Tom are you all right – you said something happened here?"

The voice of his classmate Katie snapped Tom back to reality.

"I mean in the past, I bet." he replied.

"Yeah, like human sacrifice. I knew there was a reason we brought Benny!" Quinn sniggered.

Quinn Christopher was Tom's best mate and Benny Sherwood was the school geek. Tom couldn't believe it when he was paired to work with geeky Benny.

"Being stuck with you is so lame," Tom groaned.

Suddenly, he spotted something gleaming brightly in the grass. It was a ring. He picked it up and it began to glow. Tom recognized it instantly as a Magical object and knew he had to keep it out of sight. But it was too late!

"Wow! Look at that!" Benny grabbed the ring and instantly the glow died.

On the flight deck of an alien ship, the deafening alarms, which had been sounding since Tom had picked up the object, suddenly ceased.

"We have lost the trace," said a grotesque-looking female alien named Lexi.

A booming voice ordered Varg, the alien standing beside her, to investigate further.

"But father, I found the Magic…"

"And Varg is my first-born. He will be King. And you, Lexi, will not," yelled the voice of The Nekross King.

Down on Earth, Benny and Tom continued to argue about the strange ring.

"It's a piece of junk!"

"No. It was glowing," Benny argued.

A few steps away Miss Webster fumbled to answer her mobile phone, blissfully unaware that this was the connection to Earth the Nekross needed! As the teacher walked behind the stones to chat, the Nekross locked on to the frequency and dispatched a piece of deadly alien technology – The Voolox.

The class, busy measuring the stones, noticed nothing, as a robotic blue spine materialized on Miss Webster's back, gripping her shoulders and chest and locking on to her skull. The teacher was now under total control of Varg the Nekross – allowing them to see Earth through her eyes. They forced her to look right and left, scanning for the slightest trace of Magic. Finding nothing, she shepherded the unsuspecting children back towards the coach. The strange ring nestled in Benny's pocket. The science-obsessed boy had insisted on taking it back to the lab for testing.

"Once you're done 'experimenting' you are going to give that back to me, right?" Tom asked.

"You said it was junk!" Benny exclaimed, passing Miss Webster and climbing onto the coach. Miss Webster's eyes bore through Benny's blazer and zoomed in on the ring, hidden beneath the fabric.

Back at King's Park School, Benny headed for the science lab while Tom phoned his gran.

"Tom. I'm spring-cleaning the Chamber of Mysteries. I don't think it's been done in five hundred years!"

Tom explained what had happened on the field trip and how the Magic-charged ring he'd found was now with Benny – an Unenchanted.

"This isn't good… I'll be there in a jiffy," Ursula said, signing off.

In the science lab, Benny looked up from his tests on the ring to see Miss Webster.

"Miss! I – I wasn't going to blow anything up this time. Honest," he stuttered.

"The energy source…Give it to me!" Varg demanded, through the teacher.

Benny looked at the ring, but didn't move. Something was most definitely wrong with Miss Webster.

"Give it to me. Or be disintegrated."

Benny snatched up the ring and dived under a lab bench, just in time to dodge the energy bolts Varg fired from the Voolox attached to Miss Webster. Blasts exploding on all sides, Benny dodged out of the door and ran. At the end of a corridor he smacked into Tom who was sauntering along with a football.

"Miss Webster! She's been taken over! By aliens!" he cried.

"What are you on?" Tom said.
"Just give me the ring."

Benny barely had time to answer before another explosion shook the corridor. Tom span around to see Miss Webster, Voolox weapons engaged, heading straight for them. The boys fled down corridors,

through classrooms and cloakrooms. Words rushed out of Benny's mouth as they ran.

"That thing on her back? It's controlling her and firing lasers. No way is that Earth technology… and what about this? It glowed remember? I bet this is alien too."

Frustrated and angry Benny waved the ring at Tom, who grabbed it from him. The ring immediately glowed in Tom's hand. Benny was horrified. Was Tom also an alien?

Suddenly, Miss Webster appeared and they were forced into the gym. Now they were trapped and Miss Webster was training the Voolox weapons on them.

"We're going to die!" screeched Benny But Tom had made his mind up.

"Not while I'm here," he said, stepping forward, raising one hand and clicking his fingers.

"Kadra-dach dah!"

A fiery shield of Magical light exploded from Tom's palm enveloping the boys in a multi-coloured swirl of impenetrable energy. Benny's eyes nearly popped out of his head as the light shield absorbed the Voolox's laser beams.

In the Nekross ship the King could barely contain himself.

"The Magic! I must have it! The Nekross shall feast!" he boomed.

Lexi bowed and hit a button, releasing Miss Webster. It was time to finish the job herself.

Tom and Benny dashed out of the gym with Benny yelling questions at Tom about what he'd witnessed. Tom took a deep breath.

"It was Magic, Benny – I'm a wizard."

"No way would anyone but an alien think I'd fall for something like that! A wizard?

I'd fall for something like that! A wizard? Yeah, right! There's no such thing as Magic."

"It's better you don't believe me," said Tom. "But I'm not from another planet."

"No. That would be me," came a chilling voice behind them.

The boys turned to find Lexi, Princess of Nekron aiming her blaster at them.

"Now that definitely is an alien," Benny murmured.

"We are the Nekross, from the planet Nekron in the Korbol Galaxy. We have come for Magic!" Lexi pronounced.

"Have this on me!" Tom cried, clicking his fingers. Nothing happened; he had used his three daily spells, wasting two on homework and one on his alarm clock! Luckily, before Lexi could act, Ursula arrived, brandishing her cane, the amber stone glowing.

"I am Ursula, seventh daughter of a seventh daughter of the Magical Line of Crowe. My family have slain demons and destroyed armies of the Neverside. Whatever world you come from beware."

It was a brave speech from Tom's protective gran, but Lexi simply grinned.

"More Magic. I shall take you both!" she smiled, pressing a button on her wrist device.

Benny watched spellbound as the alien, Tom and his Gran were surrounded by rings of white energy, then disappeared.

"They've been beamed up!"

Tom and Ursula found themselves with Lexi in the arrival chamber of the starship Zarantulus. Despite their fear, they couldn't help marveling as they looked out of the window across star-strewn space towards the curve of the earth. The moment was ruined by Lexi's shrill, mocking tones.

"Earth looks so small. So far away. Say goodbye to it wizards!"

The pair were led onto the flight deck and ordered to bow to the Nekross King by Varg. Tom refused.

"If you're so important, why don't you show your face?" Tom mocked. With a burst of gas, the doors of the King's Chamber parted to reveal the most revolting sight.

The King was a gigantic, slimy mass of bubbling, wart-covered blubber. Varg and Lexi knelt before their hideous father. "Hail the might of Nekron!"

Varg addressed the prisoners. "Consider yourselves privileged. It is not our father's custom to grant an audience with his herd."
"We're human, not cattle!" Tom said, mustering every ounce of his courage.
"And I might be old. But I'm no cow. I am Ursula, of the Magical Line of Crowe and I will smite thee with Magic."

"Maa-kraak dah!" Ursula banged her cane on the floor and aimed it at the King, sending Magical energy flying towards him. Unbelievably, this awesome power didn't seem to hurt him, instead, he absorbed it.

"Delicious!" He roared, licking his fleshy lips.

The same thing happened when Ursula used her second and third spells to blast Magic towards Varg and Lexi.

"They're feeding on it!" Tom cried, "They're feeding on Magic!"

"Then we're powerless," Ursula sighed, dropping her cane. "Magic is all we've got."

Tom hugged his gran tight and the two wizards listened in horror as Varg explained that the Nekross had sucked every planet and star dry of Magic.

"There's no Magic left in the universe?" Ursula whispered.

"Only on Earth," laughed the King "and now we shall feast on that!"

Tom seized his chance. "Feast on this!" he cried, drop-kicking his football straight at the King and pulling his gran after him.

"Run, Gran!" he yelled and the pair hurtled down a corridor with the King's angry roars echoing in their ears.

Racing through the ship they hastily retraced their steps and found themselves back in the arrival chamber. Tom couldn't believe his luck. They could beam themselves back the way they'd came. He pulled a lever and the teleport beam appeared just as Varg, Lexi and the Nekross guards burst in.

Ursula stepped forward to protect Tom, letting go of his hand just as Tom stepped into the light beam… and vanished.

Tom reappeared in the locker corridor, just behind Benny.

"They've still got my Gran!" Tom cried, running for home, with Benny hard on his heels.

"I'm going back, I'm going to save her… If she's still alive."

Ursula was alive, but a helpless captive. In the next cell were two other wizards who'd been captured at the stone circle and drained of Magic.

"Look what they did to my son!" said one, gesturing to a wrinkled old man beside him.

The Magic extraction had also sucked all the life from the boy – leaving him an old man. Ursula sank down in a corner, heartbroken. Back on Earth Tom was urging Benny to forget what he'd seen and go home.

"What?" Benny cried, incredulous. "I just saw an alien, I just saw one of our teachers get taken over by aliens. Your Gran got abducted by aliens. And, oh yes, you turn out to be a Magician."

"Wizard." Tom corrected.

"You can't leave me behind. These are aliens, Tom. That's not hocus-pocus – it's science. You need me!"

Tom reluctantly allowed Benny to follow him home.

"You don't tell anyone. Understand? Not about the aliens. Not about the Magic." Tom warned Benny, as they stood in the hall of his home.

"What would aliens with the technology to travel light years, want with Magic?" Benny asked.

"They feed on it."

"That makes sense. Whatever you call 'Magic', it's an energy. Organisms live on energy."

Tom took out the Ring of Healing and explained that a wizard must have lost it when the Nekross took him. Enchanted with the wizard's Magic, it would still be connected to

him – as if with an invisible cord. Benny realised that they could use this connection to trace the wizard and Ursula back to the starship Zarantulus.

Benny was puzzled when Tom opened the door to a downstairs loo, then knocked twice on it before saying –

"Chamber of Crowe, open to me, reveal yourself on the knock of three."

With a third rap, Tom opened the door to reveal… a long passageway of ancient stone lit by flickering torches, which led into a cave filled with Magical apparatus and spell books – The Chamber of Mysteries.

"A parallel dimension?" asked Benny.
"It's Magic," Tom said. "Does your toilet vanish when you knock on the door and say an enchantment?"

Suddenly the Chamber was plunged into darkness, before the candles flickered once more, revealing a little man with a crooked nose and enormous ears…

"What is that?" Benny cried.

"What? What? 'What'll be Randal Moon, Guardian of the Chamber. You imps have no business here!" Randal Moon lunged, but Tom stepped forward.

"Stop, I'm the grandson of Ursula, daughter of the Magical Line of Crowe! She's in danger and you have got to help us save her!"

"In danger? The Mistress Crowe? By the humps of Grusselbar, why didn't you be saying so before?"

Tom, still an untrained wizard, had never before entered the Chamber, so Moon had to guide him around to find the ingredients for the spell. As he worked, he angrily outlined the difference between goblins and hobgoblins – such as he – to the 'Unenchanted' Benny, while Tom explained to his science-obsessed friend that what they were making was a Passing Charm and not a matter transporter.

The last thing Benny and Tom saw before they were whisked away by the Passing Charm, was Tom's Dad, Michael, rushing into the Chamber. He did not look pleased.

"What have you done?!" Michael cried,

"No, Michael of the Unenchanted! Lay no hand on Randal Moon. Tis here an Egg of Brimstone and I'll be setting you a-sizzle!"

Michael grabbed the Egg and demanded Moon tell him exactly what was going on, but Moon rushed to the ornate scrying mirror where he saw Tom and Benny. But they weren't on the Zarantulus.

They were at the Burnt Hill Stone Circle. The charm had failed. Magic didn't work against the Nekross or their ship.

"I'm going to get them. You keep your Magical meddlings off my son!" Michael yelled, pocketing the Egg of Brimstone and running out of the Chamber.

It didn't take Tom long to realise that the charm had failed and they'd been 'bounced' elsewhere. But it was brainy Benny who worked out they could bring the Nekross to them by raising the power of the stones, just as the wizard who'd lost the ring had been doing.

"Even if I knew how, I'm out of spells until next sunrise!" groaned Tom.

Still watching the boys through the scrying mirror, Moon knew he could do the job for Tom and raise the stones' power.

As their Magic crackled, alarms once again blared on the Nekross ship, which immediately headed back to Earth to capture the wizards.

Tom and Benny grinned in delight as they saw the Zarantulus loom above them. The teleport beam appeared just as Michael, driving his 4x4 raced into the stone circle. The boys, Michael and his car were all beamed up.

Nanoseconds later they found themselves in the arrival chamber.

"Tom! You're OK! I was going out of my mind!"

Michael barely had time to hug his son before the door flew open and Varg appeared, flanked by guards.

"So, the halfling returns – just in time for dinner!"

Tom, Benny and Michael were dragged to the flight deck where they found Ursula, trapped in the Nekross Magic extractor.

"Let her go!" Tom yelled.
"I shall feast on her," the King laughed

as Tom strained forward, desperate to rescue Ursula from the extractor capsule before it could be activated.

"And you will be next, halfling."

At these words, Michael stepped defiantly forward, brandishing the Egg of Brimstone.

"No-one threatens my family!" Varg laughed.

"An egg? You threaten the Nekross with an egg?"

Cover your eyes Benny!" Tom shouted, as Michael threw the Egg at the floor.

Dazzling white light burst from the shell, blinding the Nekross just long enough for Tom to release Ursula and for the group to run to save the other captive wizards.

At last in the arrival chamber, Tom pulled the lever to activate the teleport – but the Nekross had already shut it down.

"You're Science," he told Benny.
"You figure this out!"

"I never thought I'd say this, but the only way we're going to get off this ship is with a shed load of Magic," Benny sighed.

But both Tom and Ursula had used all their spells and now the Nekross were hammering on the door.

"There must be something we can do!" Benny cried.

"Not without Magic. I'm sorry Benny – but I told you not to come," Tom said.

Michael hugged Tom "You came back for your Gran. Your mum would've been proud of you, Tom. And so am I."

All seemed lost as the Nekross cut through the door, but suddenly a tiny sliver of golden sunlight fell on Benny's face.

"Look – the sun!" Benny shouted, pointing out of the window. "Science brings you – a sunrise! We've moved around the Earth towards a new dawn."

"And we've got three more spells!" Tom cried. "Get in the car!"

With everyone in the 4x4 he took Ursula's hand.

"Dyshaa-Faa dah!"

Tom clicked his fingers and cast a powerful spell. The Magical enchantment would allow Michael's 4x4 to fly them safely back to Earth. As the Nekross burst into the chamber, the

4x4 accelerated out through the window into space. They were going home.

Back at the stones, Ursula returned the Healing Ring to the Wizard, hoping that it would help him heal his son.

"Blessed be the Source!" They said, bowing and walking away.

"Do you think the Nekross are still up there?" Benny said.

"You heard the King. They feed on Magic and there's none left anywhere else in the universe." Ursula warned.

"But we're going to stop them, right?"
"If they want Magic, I'm going to show them just what Magic can do," Tom said. "But this is about Wizards. It's not your fight."

"You're my friend. That makes it my fight," Benny vowed.

Together, they stood watching the magnificent sunset pour its golden light between the stones. It was time for Wizards to once again keep the world safe, but this time it would be different. Wizards versus Aliens. And Tom Clarke was ready.

# DO YOU SPEAK MOONISH?

Randal Moon will be a-speaking in a very special way – a way that'll be unique to Hobgoblins like him! You'll be completing his phrases most favourite and choosing wisely from the words a-written at the page's foot.

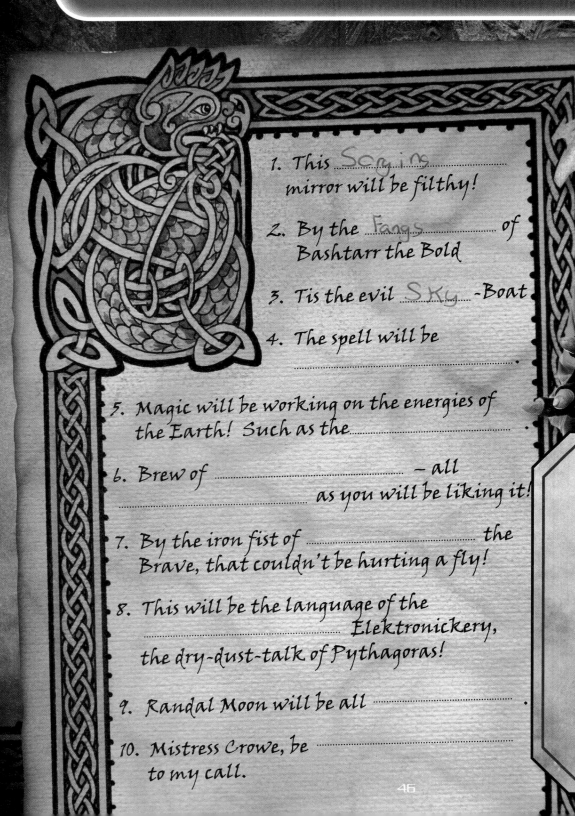

1. This _Scrying_ mirror will be filthy!

2. By the _Fangs_ of Bashtarr the Bold

3. Tis the evil _Sky_ -Boat

4. The spell will be ......................

5. Magic will be working on the energies of the Earth! Such as the ......................

6. Brew of .................... – all .................... as you will be liking it!

7. By the iron fist of .................... the Brave, that couldn't be hurting a fly!

8. This will be the language of the .................... Elektronickery, the dry-dust-talk of Pythagoras!

9. Randal Moon will be all ....................

10. Mistress Crowe, be .................... to my call.

Crescending
Fangs
Tangleweed
milksome
Sky
Hearkening
Falling Force
Scrying
Abron
Technomangers
Ears

46

# FAMILY TIES

Like any normal teenager, Tom Clarke adores his gran and would do anything to protect her. However, with them both being amongst the last Wizards in the universe, the stakes are much higher. Spot and circle ten differences between these two pictures of Tom and Ursula.

# ALIEN TECKNOCKERY

Benny is a total brainiac when it comes to technology. He might be mocked by everyone from Quinn to Randal Moon, but his technical nouse often helps save the day. Channel your inner geek by identifying the pieces of alien technology and explaining their uses.

NAME: .................................................

USE: ....................................................

.............................................................

.............................................................

.............................................................

NAME: .................................................

USE: ....................................................

.............................................................

.............................................................

.............................................................

NAME: .................................................

USE: ....................................................

.............................................................

.............................................................

.............................................................

NAME: .................................................

USE: ....................................................

.............................................................

.............................................................

.............................................................

# UNIVERSE IN A JAR

Tom, Benny, Michael and Ursula have been lucky enough to get a glimpse of deep space and now you can do the same – without ever having to meet the Nekross. Just place this cool glow-in-the-dark jar on your beside table to bring the wonders of the universe into your room every night.

## You Will Need:

- A large, clean glass jar with screw top.
- Glow-in-the-dark paint in green, blue and clear colours.
- Small bristled paint brushes (one for each colour of paint).

## What You Do:

(1)  Wash your jar thoroughly making sure it is clean, free of any labels or sticky residue.

(2)  Dry it thoroughly, inside and out.

(3)  Paint small dots of glow-in-the-dark paint all over the inside of the jar – the more imperfect the painting, the cooler it looks.

(4)  Leave to dry.

(5)  Display in a very dark room for full effect.

# UNLIKELY FRIENDSHIP

Tom and Benny are an unlikely pair of friends - the star of the school football team and the geeky, gadget-loving brainiac. Do you have an unlikely friend? Use the space below to write down all the reasons you get on. Write down some of the adventures you've had together and the times you've got each other out of trouble.

"TYPICAL. I FINALLY GET A FRIEND, AND HE GETS ME EATEN BY ALIENS."

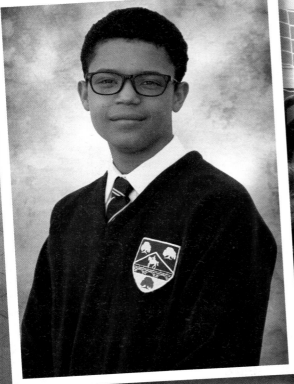

# "I THOUGHT GEEKY STUFF WAS BORING, BUT YOU ARE ROCKING IT NOW BENNY!"

KING'S PARK SECONDARY SCHOOL

# PART 2

# BENNY'S BIG QUIZ

So you aced Part 1 – let's hope so! Part II is all about the alien threat and is designed to help you avoid ending up at the sharp end of a Grazlax horn. Pick up a pen or a quill and get ready to test your outer-space smarts.

(1) The Nekross survive on a diet of…

    (a) Humans. ( )
    (b) Wizards. ( )
    (c) Magic. ( )

(2) The Skorpulus can be found…

    (a) Inside the barrel of Varg's blaster. ( )
    (b) in a hidden chamber in the floor of the Flight Deck. ( )
    (c) inside the Nekross King's mouth. ( )

(3) The Nekross King favours Varg because…

    (a) he is the first born and heir to the Nekross throne. ( )
    (b) he is a clever strategist. ( )
    (c) he always gives up his portion of Magic to his father. ( )

(4) What is the Nekross King's major weakness?

    (a) He is allergic to humans. ( )
    (b) He dissolves at the touch of water. ( )
    (c) He cannot move from his chamber on the ( )
        Zarantulus because he is grotesquely fat.

(5) The 'Brain-Scrape' has the power to…

    (a) retrieve memories. ( )
    (b) erase memories. ( )
    (c) replace memories and thoughts ( )
        with Nekross orders.

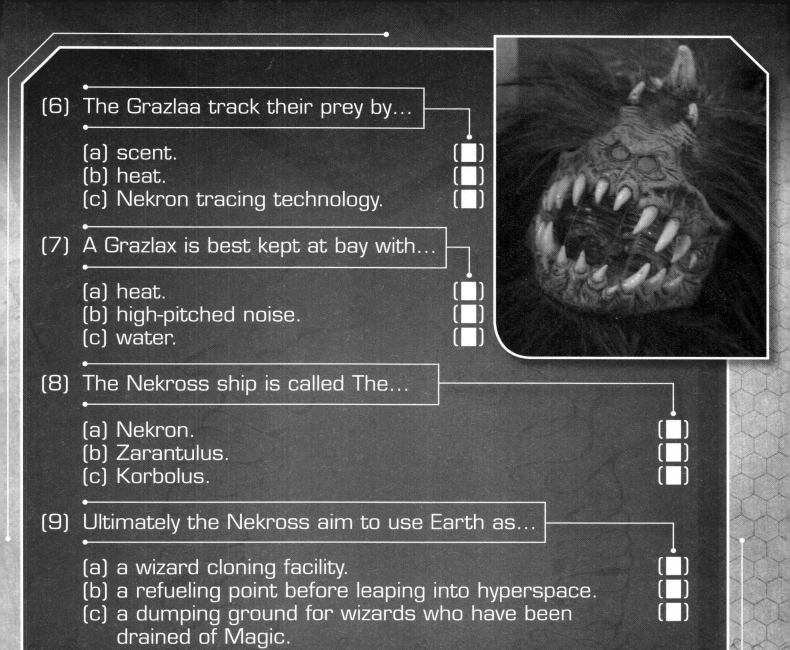

(6) The Grazlaa track their prey by...

(a) scent. [ ]
(b) heat. [ ]
(c) Nekron tracing technology. [ ]

(7) A Grazlax is best kept at bay with...

(a) heat. [ ]
(b) high-pitched noise. [ ]
(c) water. [ ]

(8) The Nekross ship is called The...

(a) Nekron. [ ]
(b) Zarantulus. [ ]
(c) Korbolus. [ ]

(9) Ultimately the Nekross aim to use Earth as...

(a) a wizard cloning facility. [ ]
(b) a refueling point before leaping into hyperspace. [ ]
(c) a dumping ground for wizards who have been [ ]
    drained of Magic.

(10) A proven way to defeat the Nekross would be to...

(a) make a spell to banish their [ ]
    ship to another part of space.

(b) dress up as Technician Jathro [ ]
    and infiltrate the flight deck of
    their ship.

(c) introduce a deadly virus into [ ]
    the Nekross ship's technology.

Answers on page 92-93

# CODED MESSAGES

Tom's been trapped by the forces of evil, but he's managed to get a message to Ursula. Can you work out how to decipher their Magical correspondence?

Ursula,

I need help and fast. Some crazed businesswoman has got me trapped in the basement below her offices. I'm tied up, so I had to use my last spell to create this message and enchant one of her Heavies, who – if you're reading this – has posted it.

Please get Benny and come and find me. Benny will need to hack into the computer system and disable the alarms. I need to get out of here before the Nektross mount their next attack!

Tom

Tom,

My beautiful boy, do not worry a moment longer, we are on our way. I had to use one of my spells on Benny's parents, because they said he had violin practice and "couldn't come out to play." Luckily I still have two left and faithful Moon is on stand-by.

Stay strong, we are with you in spirit and will have you free in no time.

Blessed be the Source,

URSULA

# CHAMBER CHALLENGE

Every young wizard needs to hone his or her powers of observation. Check out this picture of Randal Moon in the Chamber of Mysteries. You have 60 seconds to drink in every detail. When your time is up, cover the picture and try to answer the questions on the next page. No peeking!

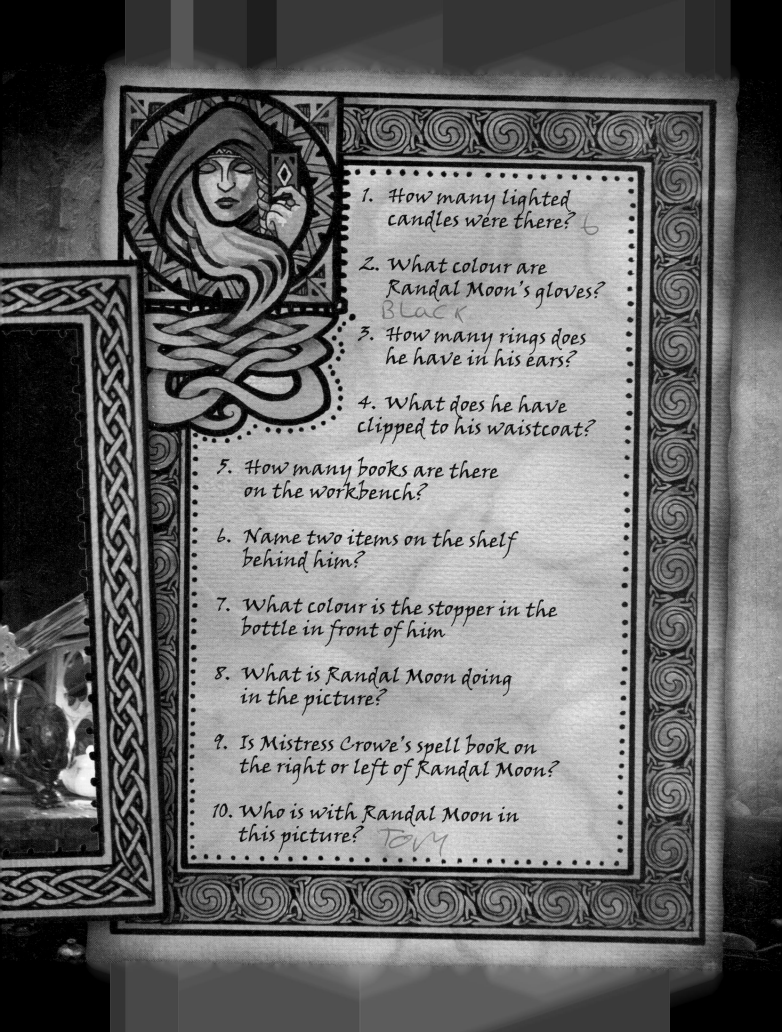

1. How many lighted candles were there? 6

2. What colour are Randal Moon's gloves?
BLACK

3. How many rings does he have in his ears?

4. What does he have clipped to his waistcoat?

5. How many books are there on the workbench?

6. Name two items on the shelf behind him?

7. What colour is the stopper in the bottle in front of him

8. What is Randal Moon doing in the picture?

9. Is Mistress Crowe's spell book on the right or left of Randal Moon?

10. Who is with Randal Moon in this picture? TOM

# BUILD A BLASTER

Varg is an awesome warrior who loves weaponry. He is always looking to update his disintegrating blaster. Use the page opposite to design him a new weapon. Don't forget to label its features.

# GRAZLAX COLOUR COPY

The Grazlax is amongst the most feared creatures in the universe, with its ability to seek out and destroy any foe. Learn to draw the terrifying alien, so you can show and forewarn other wizards who might encounter it. Copy the detail in each square of the grid, into the corresponding square opposite.

# LEX-TREME CLOSE-UP

Lexi has a real interest in the world and especially Earth culture. On a recent visit to Earth, Lexi used the scanner in her gauntlet to record some images, but it malfunctioned and zoomed in. Can you identify who she has taken the pictures of?

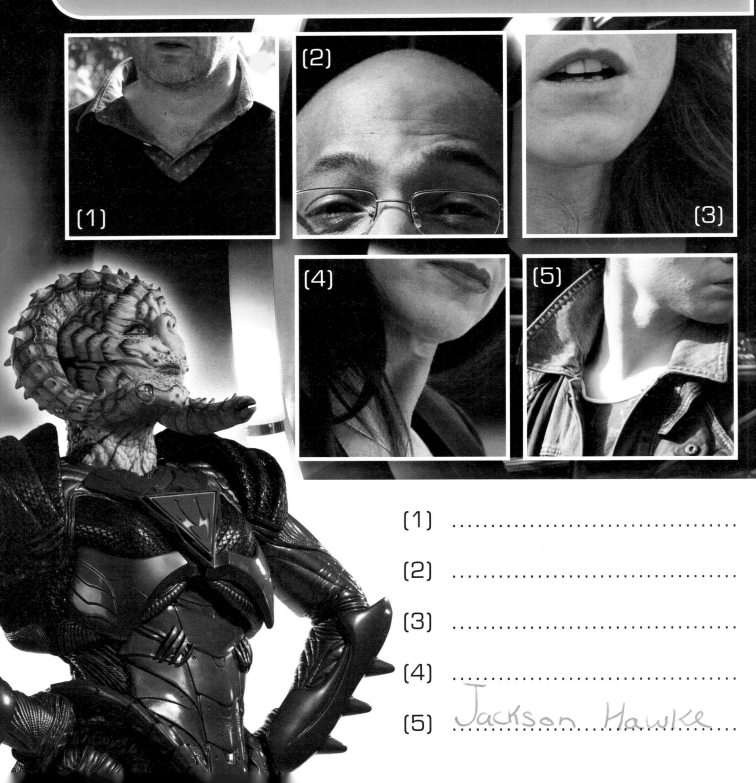

(1) ...............................

(2) ...............................

(3) ...............................

(4) ...............................

(5) Jackson Hawke

# SCRYING MIRROR ON THE WALL

The Mistress Crowe will have cast a spell wrongly and the visions in the Scrying Mirror will have been shattered. You'll be helping Randal Moon to be a-putting the picture back together!

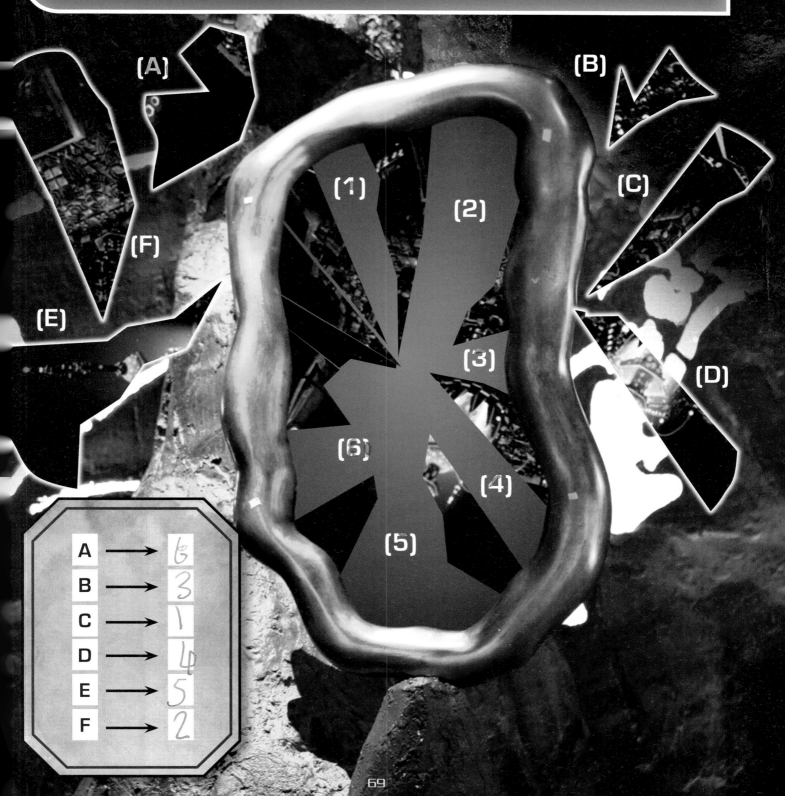

| | | |
|---|---|---|
| A | → | 6 |
| B | → | 3 |
| C | → | 1 |
| D | → | 4 |
| E | → | 5 |
| F | → | 2 |

# GRAZLAX ATTACKS

Tom and Benny were at Tom's house. Tom's gran, Ursula, had summoned him to the Chamber of Mysteries after school and he had brought Benny, the only person outside his family who knew that he was an alien-fighting wizard. The new friends had already been through a great deal – now they made their way into the cavern where Ursula worked her Magic.

"Ah! Thomas! Very good! And you brought Benny too!" Ursula exclaimed.

They received a frostier welcome from hobgoblin Randal Moon.

"Pickling Piskies! The Chamber will be infested by the Unenchanted!"

Ursula was planning a shrouding spell.

"'It'll be an enchantment to hide the Magic of wizards all around the world from the Sky-Ship. Wizards will be casting their spells with no fear of the Unworld ones a-spotting them," Moon explained.

The shrouding spell needed three wizards, channeling their Magic, Tom was delighted when Moon handed him his very own Magical robe, which he immediately pulled on.

Waving Benny back Ursula, Randal Moon and Tom held hands.

"Hear us, we'll be calling on the Source to protect the children of Magic from those beyond the star-glittery heavens... Protect us and shroud our Magic."

"Raa-shey-dah!" Tom, Ursula and Moon exclaimed in unison. Magical energy crackled around them.

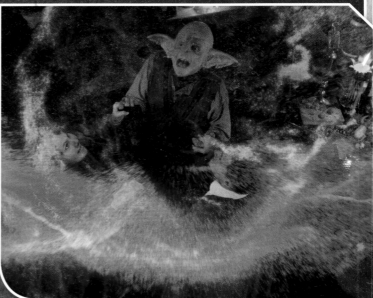

Although they now couldn't be spotted from space, they would still be vulnerable when the Nekross were on Earth.

Meanwhile, The Nekross starship Zarantulus hung menacingly in space. The Nekross King was hungry.

Luckily, Lexi had a plan. She held up a thin glass vial. "I have a stratagem to end your woes father. Tom Clarke's scent. Distilled

from surfaces he touched aboard
the Zarantulus."

At first the King did not understand, but
Lexi proudly outlined the details of her plan.

"What we need is something to track Tom
Clarke. Something that can't be stopped.
Something determined, that will stalk him,
trap him, suck the Magic from his shattered
bones and bring it to you, my father."

She ushered in two Nekross guards,
clutching a battered metal box containing
something which snarled and gnashed.

"This is a stratagem of madness!"
Varg exclaimed, stepping back from
the caged creature.

"Do it! Set the Grazlax on the boy wizard
and await his screams," the King proclaimed.

The next day was Saturday and Tom,
who had been invited over by Benny, was
walking towards his house, when he met
Katie from his school. She was delivering
leaflets for her Dad's shop and invited
Tom to join her. Tom hesitated. Katie
was very pretty, he had liked her for ages…

but he had promised Benny.

"What is with you two? You've got really
matey all of a sudden," Katie asked.

"Didn't you know? Geeks are cool!"
Tom smiled.

"The only way Benny is ever going to be
cool is sat in a snowdrift," Katie called as
she rode off.

"Watch he doesn't blow you up."

Benny's mum seemed in a
high state of excitement when
she opened the door. She
beamed at Tom and introduced
herself as Tricia. Tom could
barely hear her through the
terrible din that was coming
from inside the house.

"Benny's nearly done. That's
him practicing," she said,
ushering him inside.

They found Benny, screeching away on
the violin, under the watchful gaze of
Richard, his father. Tricia introduced Tom
to Richard who awkwardly tried to high-five
him. Tricia offered him some homemade
lemonade…

"Or fresh orange juice. Or peppermint tea?"
"Benny loves his herbal infusions,"
Tricia Sherwood proudly exclaimed.

Dying of embarrassment, Benny led
Tom outside, moaning about the difficulties
of living with pushy parents who subjected
him to music lessons, organic food and
regular quiz nights.

"Welcome to the Shed of Dread," Benny said, unlocking the padlock of a garden shed to reveal a jumble of furniture and scientific odds and ends. He tugged the cover off an object to reveal a TV.

"To you it's a telly. To mum and dad it's like the brain cell equivalent of a black hole," Benny groaned.

"So they don't know you've got this and this whole lab thing is really a cover up so you can come and watch *Total Wipeout?*" Tom grinned. "You really are a genius!"

The boys had just begun assembling some flat pack shelves when there was a thud outside.

"Did you hear something?"

"Next door's cat," Benny explained. "Mum gets fed up with it messing up her flowerbeds."

They carried on building and chatting about Benny's mathematical genius father and his plans for Benny to follow in his footsteps.

"You know I can be a genius too and put this whole place together with the click of my fingers," Tom said, and just as the poorly constructed shelving unit began to fall apart he spoke a Magical incantation. "Ein-shosh-barr dah!" In an instant the shelves and shed were in order.

"If the Nekross show up now and you're one spell down, don't say I didn't tell you!" Benny warned.

A thump from above, signaled that 'next

door's cat' was on the shed roof. They peered at the very un-cat-like shape sitting on the frosted skylight.

'SMASH!'

The skylight shattered on their heads and something dropped through it.

Tom and Benny just had time to glimpse the furry blue ball with its pointed horn, jagged mouth full of gnashing teeth and searing red eyes, before it let out a terrifying scream. This vicious little critter was the Grazlax and it had tracked and found Tom Clarke. Amid its shrieking it launched itself at the boys.

"Leg it!" Benny yelled.

They managed to get out of the shed, but the Grazlax snagged Tom's trouser leg in its jaws. Benny grabbed a garden broom and swung it wildly at the creature, trying to hit it away from his friend, but the Grazlax just grabbed onto the end of the broom instead and began to eat through it.

Benny's parents, watching through the window, had no idea that their son and his friend were being attacked by one of the most dangerous creatures in the universe.

"What are they playing at down there?" Tricia asked.

"Hockey, I think," Richard replied setting the cheese board on the table.

At the bottom of the garden, the boys launched the broom and its attached, snarling Grazlax into the shed, bolting it in.

"What is that? One of yours or one of theirs? Goblin or alien?"

"I can feel Magic in anything from the Neverside. That's alien. The Nekross have sent it. They must have." Benny padlocked the door as his dad called them both up for tea. The boys sat at the table, facing the window, keeping a wary eye on the shed, whilst trying

to make small talk with the Sherwoods who wanted to know more about their son's new friend and what he wanted to do with his life.

"Please don't say you want to be a footballer. So many young people these days want to be footballers or actors or pop stars. It's as if they have forgotten they have brains." said Mrs Sherwood.

Tom, who wanted to be a footballer, stuttered about not being sure, but then Benny came to his rescue. "Tom wants to save the world!"

Tricia Sherwood was thrilled. "Ah! An environmentalist! Tom that's brilliant!"

"We like to do our bit, don't we darling?" Richard added. "We have a sustainable multi-fuel boiler in the basement, you know!"

Tom stared out of the window. The creature was lifting the shed off its foundations. He pretended he was interested in seeing some photos so that Benny's parents would leave the room to fetch the family photo albums.

"We've got to get rid of your mum and dad," Tom whispered, "We can't let them see what's down there."

"How do we do that?" Benny asked.

"Have you got a gran? Or someone on the other side of the city, that they worry about?"

"I've got a Great Uncle Clarence, why?" There was no time for Tom to explain.

"Meesch-enfar-dah!" With a snap of his fingers and a spark of Magical energy, Tom cast his second spell of the day.

"We've had a phone call. Your Great Uncle Clarence – he's flooded the house!" said Richard, rushing in to the room.

"See you later," Tricia added, running towards the front door. "Benny don't eat too much piccalilli, you know what it does to your insides!" With that they were gone.

"When they come back maybe you can use your last spell of the day and make them – cooler?" Benny groaned.

Tom looked out of the window. The shed door was wide open. The creature had escaped! The boys rushed out of the front door to check on Benny's parents, but they were climbing into their car and the Grazlax was thankfully nowhere to be seen.

Benny breathed a sigh of relief. "At least they're safe!"

He and Tom turned to go back indoors but noticed tell-tale footprints on the step.

"It's in the house!" Tom exclaimed.

"We need a plan!" Benny said, as they tiptoed inside, following the trail which led upstairs.

"Find it. Deal with it. Then football's on the telly at three!"

"That's what wizards call a plan?" Benny said, incredulous.

"Who needs a plan when you've got Magic!" Tom replied, creeping silently upstairs with Benny close behind.

All was silent. Benny thought the creature could be hiding – more scared of them, than they were of it.

"Look, if you want to put it on a couch and ask it questions about growing up as an ankle-snapper, fine. But first we're going to

fix it so it can't bite our arms off!" Tom snapped.

A loud thump from Benny's bedroom interrupted the discussion. Gingerly pushing the door open, the boys inched inside. It was eerily quiet. Arming himself with a tennis racket, Tom lowered himself to the floor to look under the bed. Nothing.

Suddenly, the Grazlax burst out of the bed, spitting mattress stuffing from its jaws. The boys dived under the bed and attempted to fend off the snapping Grazlax with the tennis racket. It was futile. The Grazlax just bit the entire head of the racket off, strings and all, before tipping the bed over, exposing the cowering boys.

There was nothing for it.

"Maifash-andwy dah!"

Tom used his last, precious spell to summon a ball of Magical energy which sent a wicker storage basket flying towards

the Grazlax, imprisoning it, temporarily. As the Grazlax bashed up and down inside the basket, Tom desperately tried to phone his Dad.

"I don't believe it! I've got no credit!" he cried as the Grazlax's horn pierced the lid of the basket. It was getting out. He grabbed the nearest object he could find – a toy robot - and began to hammer at the puncturing horn.

"That's a Sugoi Kinzoku Robot!" Benny cried in annoyance. "It's rare!"

"You really are a geek!" Tom said, discarding the robot and picking up a large book about space.

The creature's horn went straight through the heavy tome. The Grazlax was almost free. As it burst out of the basket Tom and Benny ran and hid in Benny's parents room, pushing a chest of drawers against the door.

Benny picked up the telephone in panic, only to find the Grazlax had chewed through the phone lines. More silence followed and then Benny said…

"I think it's in the wall!"

"What, How can it be in the wall? The pair listened to the sound of chomping coming ever nearer.

"It's not in the wall – it's in the chimney!" Tom cried as the Grazlax landed in the fireplace in a cloud of soot. Tom tried in vain to trap it under a metal bin but it escaped again. The Grazlax stared at Tom, ready to pounce and devour him. Instinctively, Tom grabbed for something to use as a weapon.... a hairdryer?

But maybe the Grazlax didn't know it was just a hairdryer. He fired up the dryer and the Gralax began to back off, snapping and snarling.

On the flight deck of the Zarantulus, alarms sounded and Lexi and Varg stared anxiously at the strange readings on their instruments.

"The body temperature of the Grazlax is increasing... rapidly. I'm reading major metabolic irregularities!" Lexi cried.

Back at Benny's, Tom was still blasting the Grazlax with hot air and it was retreating into the Sherwood's en suite.

"Not such a chompy chappy now, are you?" Tom quipped. The Grazlax staggered into the bathroom and Benny slammed the door on it. Was it over?

The boys had just begun to discuss what they should do with the weakened alien creature, when a huge flash of light burst through the crack of the bathroom door. There were three, low thumps and squeals.

Tom urged Benny to open the door and investigate. "You've got the enquiring mind." "Maybe some things you don't want to know," Benny muttered.

Tom pulled Benny out of the way and opened

the door. The empty husk of the Grazlax lay wet with orange goo on the bathroom floor.

"It's like it exploded... Or something exploded out of it," Benny said. The boys peered into the bath and sure enough not one but three Grazlaa snapped and snarled back at them.

"It didn't explode," Tom cried. "It had kids!" They backed away in horror. "How can there be three of them?"

"Cellular division. Like an amoeba. They don't have to breed to multiply, they can just break apart!" Benny explained.

"The heat started a biological reaction. Like with a crocodile...They have to be a certain temperature before they can breed."

Tom had no idea what Benny was talking about but he wished the creature was a crocodile. A crocodile wouldn't be hunting them through the house at breakneck speed, destroying everything and anything in its path,

like these alien creatures were doing.

The boys raced from the bathroom, up the stairs and now found themselves barricaded in the attic. They sat down and tried to figure out what to do next.

"You know, Quinn and Katie – they think I've gone weird," noted Tom.

"Well," mused Benny, "you're a wizard. There are snappy aliens all over the house and a saucer full of spacemen who want to get fat on Magic. How weird can it get?"

Tom agreed, that the situation was indeed freaky.

"The really weird thing is I'm sort of enjoying it. Or I was 'til we got the

Gnashing Nasties trashing my house," admitted Benny.

"Do you know what really is weird? For a science freak, you're not so bad," Tom said, opening up for the first time.

"You don't understand the first thing about Magic – but I can talk to you about it and I've never had that before." Tom at last had found a friend with whom he could be his true self.

This bonding session didn't last long, as a thump from inside the water tank signaled a Grazlax had found them.

In seconds the critter has worked it's way around the attic and leapt at them from beneath a sheet-covered tailor's dummy. Tom selected a cricket bat ready to defend themselves but in the ensuing melee, Benny's old, toy jack-in-the-box tumbled to the ground emitting a high-pitched squeal. The Grazlax yelped in pain and dived back into the water tank! Tom and Benny took the opportunity to escape the attic and headed downstairs. The house was eerily empty of Grazlaa - Tom and Benny surmising that they must be in the basement where the family's eco-boiler heated the house. Grazlaa, they now knew, needed heat to multiply.

Tom and Benny's worst fears were confirmed when flashes of light and more thuds emanated from the basement. A moment later, the basement door swung open to reveal three Grazlaa, then another three, then three more! Tom threw the cricket bat at them and he and Benny dashed upstairs with the creatures in pursuit. Suddenly, the shrill ring of the doorbell filled the air. The creatures writhed in pain until, unable to bear it, one of them gnashed into the doorbell, causing it to spark and go silent.

"Hello? Benny? Tom?"

It was Katie. Benny wasn't sure he'd locked the door and if Katie opened it she'd be history. Benny bravely distracted the Grazlaa, while Tom answered the door. Katie invited him to go for pizza with her but Tom explained he couldn't let Benny down.

"He's lucky having you as a friend," Katie smiled, heading off. Tom badly wanted to follow her, but he had work to do.

On the Zarantulus, Lexi faced the wrath of the King as she realised the Grazlaa would soon multiply into millions and destroy everything on Earth.

"I sought only to use the Grazlax to rid ourselves of the boy wizard. Instead I have destroyed the last source of Magic in the universe," Lexi agonised.

Varg proudly announced his plan to save the day. They would destroy the house and the area around it with a blast from the ion pulse cannon.

"Put the Zarantulus into full battle mode!" the Nekcross King cried.

Meanwhile Benny had trapped all the Grazlaa in the basement. Sadly, the proximity to his Dad's eco-boiler meant the cellar was now full of Grazlaa. Tom thought for a moment. High-pitched noise seemed to hurt them. Within seconds he'd found an operatic CD and put it in the stereo. Grabbing a speaker each, Tom and Benny gave the basement a blast of soprano.

The Grazlaa screamed in pain but then one of them ripped out a fuse in the fuse box – the speakers fell silent. The boys had to flee. In desperation they shut themselves into the music room. They were trapped. If they escaped out of the window, they'd unleash the Grazlaa on the world and they'd destroy everything! Suddenly, Tom spotted Benny's violin. Handing it to Benny, he grabbed his phone, tapping the amp app he used for his electric guitar.

"What? I can't play this!" Benny said.

"That's the point!"

"You're right! And if we keep the mic and your phone close, we'll get feedback too – the Larsen Effect!"

"I don't care what it's called, but double the screeching sounds good to me!"

Hovering just outside Earth's atmosphere, the Nekross trained their ion pulse cannon directly at Benny's house and engaged its awesome power.

"Maximum pulse in five… four… three…" Varg announced.

Unaware of the threat from above, Benny began to play his violin, working up through a scale until his bow screeched on an excruciatingly piercing note. Tom aimed his phone amp at the Grazlaa and they staggered back, cried out and exploded.

Eruption after eruption spattered the pair in bright orange goo as the creatures burst and popped one after the other! Within seconds, not one remained and Tom and Benny were drenched from head to foot.

Watching their screens, the Nekross suddenly noticed the Grazlaa had been destroyed. Varg quickly stopped the countdown - Earth and its delicious Magic was safe. The Zarantulus retreated to the dark side of the Moon.

"What am I going to tell my parents?" Benny murmured, surveying the devastation.

Luckily, Tom had one more idea. Minutes later, his grandmother Ursula arrived at the house. Convinced this was the work of Bogles from the Neverside, she nevertheless agreed to help. She held her cane aloft and…

"Spree-falow dah!"

The house was replaced by a huge bouncy castle. She tried again.

"Spree-fasha-allah dah!" This time a huge, house-shaped cake sat in its place! Ursula reassured Benny she'd get it right with her third spell…

"Sprash-afalla-waan dah!"

The house was as it had been before the Grazlaa attacked – well almost. The Sherwood's reproduction Ming vase may have been replaced by the priceless real thing, but hopefully no-one would notice!

# IMAGINE THE SKORPULUS

It's big, it's bad and it's lurking beneath you! No-one has ever seen the Skorpulus and lived to tell the tale. What do you see when it enters your nightmares? Draw what you imagine it to look like here.

# MR. SHERWOOD'S SUDOKU

Benny's father is a mathematical genius who's intent on seeing his only son follow in his footsteps to Trinity College Oxford. He's devised this number puzzle for Benny – but Benny's too busy helping Tom fight aliens to do it. Can you complete it for Benny and keep his Dad off his back?

|   | 6 | 7 | 9 | 5 | 8 |   |   | 4 |
|---|---|---|---|---|---|---|---|---|
| 9 | 1 | 3 |   |   | 4 |   | 2 |   |
|   |   | 8 | 3 |   | 1 | 7 | 6 | 9 |
| 3 |   |   | 6 | 8 |   | 4 |   | 1 |
| 7 | 8 | 1 |   | 3 |   | 6 | 5 | 2 |
| 6 |   | 2 |   | 7 | 5 |   |   | 8 |
| 8 | 3 | 9 | 5 |   | 7 | 2 |   |   |
|   | 2 |   | 8 |   |   | 5 | 4 | 7 |
| 5 |   |   | 2 | 1 | 6 | 9 | 8 |   |

You need to ensure each horizontal line, vertical line and 3x3 box in the grid contains the numbers 1 – 9.

# ODD ONE OUT

Tom thinks he's found a new soul mate in Jackson Hawke, but could this new friendship lead him into dangerous situations? Which of these images of Tom and Jackson is the odd one out?

WRITE YOUR
ANSWER HERE

The odd one out is D

# COSMIC CROSSWORD

You'll be thrown into the Skorpulus' pit if you can't complete this crossword about the mighty Nekross.

## Across

[3] Area of the Zarantulus where Lexi and Varg steer and control the ship (6,4)

[4] "The Nekross shall _ _ _ _ _!" Favourite Nekross saying when they are confident of capturing a Wizard and extracting some Magic (5)

[8] Chair or seat occupied by a sovereign or exalted being (6)

[9] Name of this character (6)

[10] When Ursula and Tom laid eyes on the Nekross King they _ _ _ _ _ _ in horror. (6)
Meaning they drew in their breath in shock and horror!

[12] Varg is _ _ _ _ to the Nekron throne. (4)

[14] Intergalactic vehicle used by aliens (9)

## Down

[1] Galactic gun-like weapon favoured by Varg (7)

[2] Units of measurement used by the Nekross to measure the amount of Magic extracted (11)

[5] Planet inhabited by humans and wizards (5)

[6] Colour of Varg and Lexi's armoured uniforms (4)

[7] Varg finds himself next to these Egyptian architectural wonders, when banished by Jackson Hawke (8)

[10] When Varg displeases his father he _ _ _ _ _ _ _ to obtain his forgiveness and favour (7)

[11] Growths or lumps on the skin of the Nekross King (5)

[13] "_ _ _ _ the might of Nekron!" (4)

**3** [ ][ ][ ][ ][ ][ ][ ][ ]

**4** F R a s t **6** [ ]

**8** [ ][ ][ ][ ]

**9** j a t h r c

**10** G a s p l d

**11** [ ]

**12** [ ][ ][ ][ ]

**13** [ ]

**14** [ ][ ][ ][ ][ ]

# BENNY'S BIG QUIZ

# PART 3

Here's where things get serious, this is no true or false or multi-choice test. You're going to have to scrape your brain to recall everything you've learnt so far about wizardkind and the alien threat. Pick up your pen and get writing – as Tom would say, 'football's on in a minute!'

(1) Where in the universe do the Nekross hail from?

(2) What Magical item did Ursula bequeath Helen?

(3) What is Jathro's full rank?

(4) What do the Nekross call human wizards like Tom Clarke?

(5) What happens to wizards once they've had their Magic extracted by the Nekross?

(6) Which portable Magical item does Ursula possess which allows her to communicate with Moon?

(7) How could you tell Varg and Lexi apart?

(8) What dark secret does Jackson Hawke have in his past?

(9) What does Benny call his garden-based 'lab' where he does experiments and watches TV?

(10) Where does Ursula's Magical amber reside?

(11) When Lexi changed into a human what was her name?

(12) How did Lexi get friendly with Tom, while on Earth?

(13) Name one of the defeated foes of the Nekross?

(14) What does Michael Clarke do for a living?

(15) What type of Magical tea does Ursula prefer?

Answers on page 92-93

# BORED GAME

Jackson Hawke is feeling bored and wants to make mischief with his 'Brother in Magic' Tom. Help them play this game. Grab a dice and your BFF, then cut the character counters from the answers page. Youngest player begins.

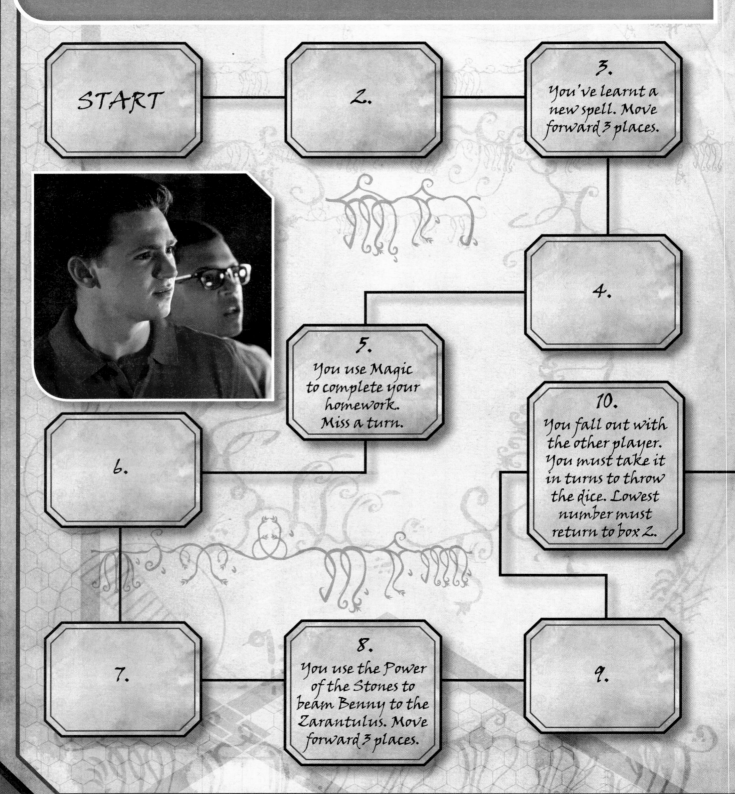

**START**

**2.**

**3.**
You've learnt a new spell. Move forward 3 places.

**4.**

**5.**
You use Magic to complete your homework. Miss a turn.

**6.**

**10.**
You fall out with the other player. You must take it in turns to throw the dice. Lowest number must return to box 2.

**7.**

**8.**
You use the Power of the Stones to beam Benny to the Zarantulus. Move forward 3 places.

**9.**

**14.**

**15.**

**16.**
You use Grim Magic to get a free takeaway pizza. Go back 2 boxes.

**13.**
Create and say a new spell and move forward 2 boxes.

**17.**

**18.**
You use Magic to beat some bullies. Take another turn.

**12.**
You use Grim Magic to banish Varg and his cronies to the Amazon rainforest. Move forward 2 boxes but throw an even number to continue.

**19.**
Move forward 1 box if you can complete the wizard phrase to give thanks for Magic. "Blessed be the _____!"

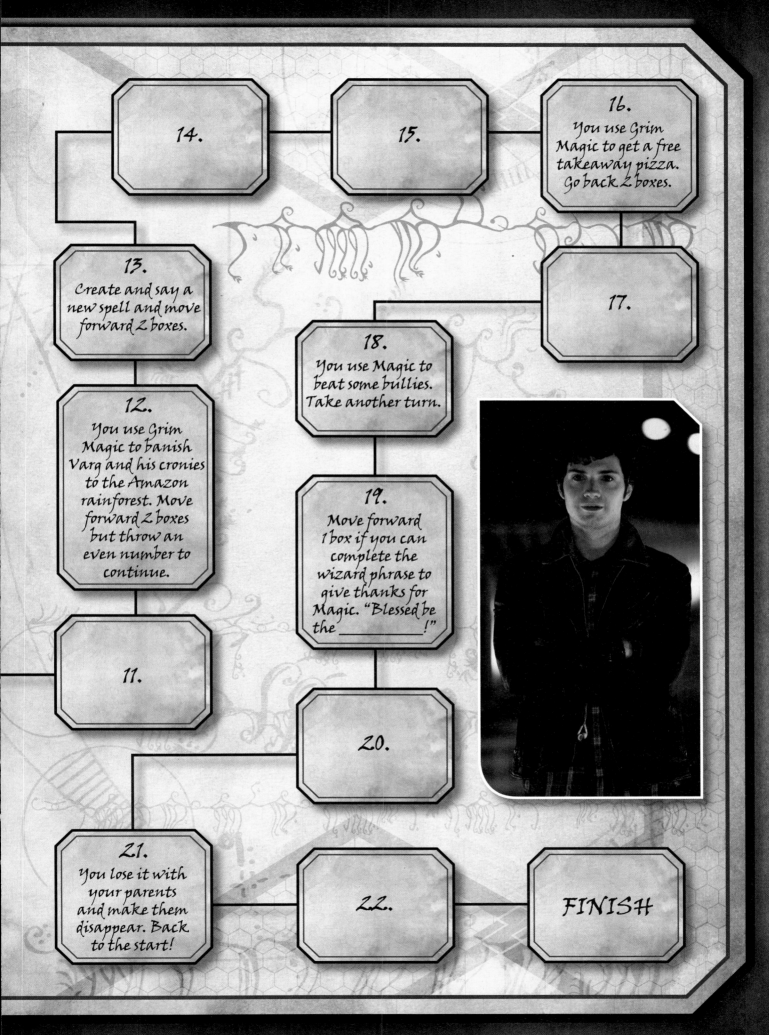

**11.**

**20.**

**21.**
You lose it with your parents and make them disappear. Back to the start!

**22.**

**FINISH**

# THE NEXT CHAPTER

Can't wait for the next installment of Wizards vs Aliens? What would you like to happen next? Use these pages to write the next chapter in Tom Clarke's story and then dream up and draw him a new and fearsome alien foe.

Magic

Magic

I Magic

I'm a wizard & can't you I tell you I

Need majic!

# ANSWERS

## P 30 – 31 _ Benny's Big Quiz – Part I
1. False - they only have 3 a day.
2. False - he comes from the Magical Line of Crowe.
3. True.
4. True.
5. False - there is a Magical Chamber in Tom's house, but it's accessible via the downstairs toilet.
6. True.
7. False – Randal Moon is being a Hobgoblin, Hob Hob Hob!
8. False - he calls her 'Mistress Crowe'.
9. False - they see through an enchanted Scrying Mirror.
10. False - it's called Stonescript.
11. True.
12. False - they do return to warn people, but as 'Pale Shadows' not ghosts.
13. True.
14. False - Earth at risk because it's the only planet in the universe with Magic (the Nekross having sucked the Magic from every other planet and star in the universe.

## P 32 – 33 _ Wizards Wordsearch

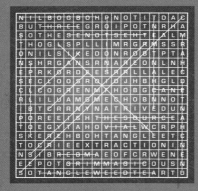

The extra word is EXTRACTION

## P 34 – 35 _ Who Said It?
1. Lexi
2. Gaunt
3. Nekross King
4. Tom Clarke
5. Randal Moon
6. Ursula Crowe
7. Benny Sherwood
8. Varg
9. Jackson Hawke
10. Michael Clarke

## P 46 _ Do You Speak Moonish?
1. Scrying
2. Fangs
3. Sky
4. Crescending
5. Falling Force
6. Tangleweed; milksome
7. Abron
8. Technomages
9. Ears
10. Hearkening

## P 53 _ Family Ties

## P 55 _ Amazing Alien Tecknockery
1. Nekross Magic Extractor
2. Nekross Teleport Beam
3. Nekross Form Filter
4. The Brain Scrape
5. Cyborg Voolox

## P 58 – 59 _ Benny's Big Quiz Part II
1. [c]
2. [b]
3. [a]
4. [c]
5. [a]
6. [a]
7. [b]
8. [b]
9. [a]
10. [c]

## P 60 – 61 _ Coded Messages

Gran,

I need help and fast. Some crazed businesswoman has got me trapped in the basement below her offices. I'm tied up, so I had to use my last spell to create this message and enchant one of her heavies, who - if you're reading this - has posted it. Please get Benny and come and find me. Benny will need to hack into the computer system and disable the alarms. I need to get out of here before the Nekross mount their next attack!

Tom

## P 62 – 63 _ Chamber Challenge

1. 6
2. Black
3. 6
4. A watch chain
5. 9
6. Skull, books, candles, jar
7. Green
8. Making a spell
9. Right
10. Tom

## P 68 _ Lex-treme Close-up

1. Michael Clarke
2. Richard Sherwood
3. Helen Clarke
4. Stephanie Gaunt
5. Jackson Hawke

## P 69 _ Scrying Mirror on the Wall

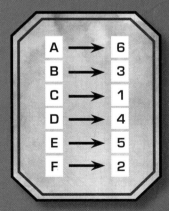

A → 6
B → 3
C → 1
D → 4
E → 5
F → 2

## P 82 _ Mr. Sherwood's Sudoku

| 2 | 6 | 7 | 9 | 5 | 8 | 1 | 3 | 4 |
| 9 | 1 | 3 | 7 | 6 | 4 | 8 | 2 | 5 |
| 4 | 5 | 8 | 3 | 2 | 1 | 7 | 6 | 9 |
| 3 | 9 | 5 | 6 | 8 | 2 | 4 | 7 | 1 |
| 7 | 8 | 1 | 4 | 3 | 9 | 6 | 5 | 2 |
| 6 | 4 | 2 | 1 | 7 | 5 | 3 | 9 | 8 |
| 8 | 3 | 9 | 5 | 4 | 7 | 2 | 1 | 6 |
| 1 | 2 | 6 | 8 | 9 | 3 | 5 | 4 | 7 |
| 5 | 7 | 4 | 2 | 1 | 6 | 9 | 8 | 3 |

## P 83 – Odd One Out

D

## Page 84 – 85 _ Cosmic Crossword

## P 86 – 87 _ Benny's Big Quiz Part III

1. The Planet Nekron in the Korbol galaxy.
2. An amulet with an amber stone which focused her Magic and retained her memories.
3. Technician Jathro Fifteen of sub-section Alpha Grex Nine.
4. Halflings.
5. They become old.
6. A hand mirror.
7. Varg's armoured suit has spikes at the shoulders, while Lexi's doesn't. Lexi's nose is also bigger, with a pronounced inverted 'V' marking.
8. Jackson used Grim Magic to make his parents disappear, when they became too irritating.
9. The 'Shed of Dread'.
10. In the handle of her cane.
11. Lucy.
12. She pretended to be a football scout who spotted his talent.
13. The Android armies of Dokkaben; the Royal Court of Orion Five.
14. He's a vet.
15. Tanglewood tea.

## P 88 – 89 _ Bored Game
Cut-out counters